MANKY
MONKEY

MANKY
MONKEY

written by Jeanne Willis
with pictures by Tony Ross

Andersen Press
LONDON

Text copyright © 2002 by Jeanne Willis. Illustration copyright © 2002 by Tony Ross
This paperback edition first published in 2004 by Andersen Press Ltd. The rights of Jeanne Willis and Tony Ross
to be identified as the author and illustrator of this work have been asserted by them in accordance
with the Copyright, Designs and Patents Act, 1988. First published in Great Britain in 2002 by
Andersen Press Ltd., 20 Vauxhall Bridge Road, London SW1V 2SA. Published in Australia
by Random House Australia Pty., 20 Alfred Street, Milsons Point, Sydney, NSW 2061.
All rights reserved. Colour separated in Switzerland by Photolitho AG, Zürich.
Printed and bound in Italy by Grafiche AZ, Verona.

10 9 8 7 6 5 4 3 2

British Library Cataloguing in Publication Data available.

ISBN 1 84270 329 3

This book has been printed on acid-free paper

There was a Manky Monkey
Who lived up in a tree–

And he was sad, because he wasn't
Who he ought to be.

He ought to like bananas, nuts
And leaves and grubs and grapes,
But his tastes were very different
From his relatives, the apes.

He sat up in a treetop
And heaved a hefty sigh,
"I don't belong up here," he said,
"And yet I don't know why."

He tried to tell his cousin
Who just sat and scratched his fleas.
"You're bored," he said. "That's all," he said.
"Try swinging by your knees!"

The Manky Monkey tried,
But it did not improve his mood—

His aunts and uncles twice removed
Were childish and rude.
They made such silly noises,
They just chattered and they played,
They never thought important things
Like 'How the World Was Made'.

And when our Monkey told them
Of the angel in his dream,
They dangled him by both his legs
And dropped him in the stream.

At first, he feared that he would drown
But found that he could stand!

Supported by the water,
He could walk upon the sand.

Not like a monkey on all-fours,
But on his own two feet,
He put his best foot forward
And wandered down the street.

Feeling somewhat shivery
And shaky from his swim,
He sewed himself some palm leaf shorts
Which rather suited him.

He found a cave inside a hill
And made himself at home,

He gave himself the closest shave
And gave his hair a comb.

Then, feeling rather peckish,
He caught himself a fish,

And made a fire and cooked it
In a clay pot for a dish.

"I don't know who I am," he said,
"But this I know, for sure,
I'm not a monkey now
And I was never one before!"

He was lonely on his own,
But he amused himself
Inventing things, like words and wheels,
And putting up a shelf.

Then just as he was wishing
For a friend to have and hold,
Another little Manky Monkey
Came in from the cold.

She'd dreamed about an angel
And she spoke of death and life,
And he loved her very dearly
Like a husband loves his wife.

They had a billion little ones

And when those children grew,

Their children all had children—

And . . . the cutest one was YOU!

Other titles written by Jeanne Willis
and illustrated by Tony Ross:

"One of the classic picture book partnerships" *Achuka*

The Boy Who Lost His Bellybutton

Don't Let Go!

I Hate School

I Want To Be A Cowgirl

Misery Moo

Sloth's Shoes

Susan Laughs

Tadpole's Promise

What Did I Look Like When I Was A Baby?

~   ~   ~

And don't miss . . .

the Dr Xargle series including

Dr Xargle's Book of Earthlets

. . . from the same partnership!